A MIGHTY FORTRESS

A MIGHTY FORTRESS

A SCIENCE FICTION NOVELLA

RAYMUND EICH

Cover art: ID 39160854 © 1971yes | Dreamstime.com

Cover design, book design, and aircraft carrier logo are copyrights, trademarks, or trade dress of CV-2 Books.

ISBN 978-0-9991016-8-1

Second CV-2 Books trade paperback edition: February 2024

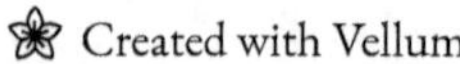 Created with Vellum

A MIGHTY FORTRESS

Theodore woke from suspended animation as if the forty-three year journey passed in a single night. Spidery robotic arms at his bedside tended his body with cold injections and warm blankets. A smooth feminine voice spoke from a speaker hidden in the low ceiling. "Welcome, Theodore."

"Melli." His voice croaked. "We're here?"

"We're in a Kuiper-type belt about four billion miles from '85." A heart rate monitor thumped a slow rhythm. "Your post-awakening assessments will take about two hours. May I suggest you enter a virtual environment? The others will join you shortly."

"Yes." Hidden behind Theodore, a robot nestled a transcranial stim helmet on his head. His heart pumped faster as the suspan chamber fell away.

A virtual simulation of *Melanchthon*'s chapel surrounded him. Fifty feet by eighty, the chapel floor visibly curved up under the cloth-draped altar. The wall of sand-colored bricks behind the altar held a float-mounted cross. Below and to the sides of the cross, like the robbers on Golgotha, hung two video screens.

Theodore followed the plush beige carpet between the pews. *Melanchthon*'s rotation pressed his avatar's feet to the floor at point-six-eight gees. His gaze jumped from screen to screen. Warmth glowed in his chest and bubbled through his smile. On the left screen, a medium shot: a glowing red ball, the red dwarf star Lalande 21185, 8.6 light years from Earth, and near it a tiny semicircle. The right screen showed a closeup. Not a semicircle: a planet half sunlit and half shaded. On the lighted side, impact craters pocked stretches of smoother terrain. The surface features rendered jagged the terminator, the dividing line between day and night.

Given the planet's close orbit to '85, the terminator would never move. Its sun would always hang low in the sky over the habitable zone. Imagine a house on the rim of a deep blue circular lake facing an eternal sunrise....

He closed his eyes. His fingers tingled. With hard but righteous work, they would build a new world—

They? "Melli, where are the others?"

Before the ship answered, sapphire sparkles heralded someone's avatar. William, the expedition's CEO. His avatar wore khakis and a deep blue polo shirt stretched over his belly. The shirt bore the rose-cross-and-starship logo used in his fundraising trips to Lutheran audiences from Stuttgart to St. Paul to Sydney. He studied the right-hand screen, then laughed and laid his paw of a hand on Theodore's shoulder. "New Augsburg at last. And as it should be, we're the first to see it."

"Not alone the first," Jonas said. His deep-set brown eyes regarded them and he walked their way on narrow feet. His reversed collar contrasted with his somber black shirt and pants. "Unless you prefer our expedition's senior pastor be excluded from this moment?"

"No, no, of course not, Reverend," William said. To Theodore, he quirked up his eyebrow. Senior pastor, yes, and respected as such; but not liked. Jonas had received a last-minute appointment to the mission as a result of some inter-faction horse-trading on the Lutheran Interstellar Terraforming Society's board of directors.

Theodore lacked any urge to know the details. He did politics when necessary, and showered afterwards.

Jonas stood between them and peered at the left-hand screen. "Why did *Melanchthon* wake us so far from the planet?"

William rolled his eyes, then turned toward a stained-glass image of Simon helping the Savior carry the Cross.

"New Augsburg lacks an atmosphere," Theodore said. His voice reminded him of teaching undergrads while earning his Ph.D. "Lalande 21185 burned much hotter when this system formed and boiled off the planet's volatiles. The gas giants are too few and too small and failed to direct comets inward. Now *Melanchthon* must."

Sapphire sparkled throughout the room. Dozens, scores, of avatars watched the screen, or the three men in the aisle.

Jonas scowled. "I know all that." He glanced around the chapel and straightened his back. "Everyone's avatar will soon be here. I must prepare for the convocation." He nodded to William and Theodore, then trod toward the altar.

Theodore sniffed out a breath. "I've explained the science a dozen times—"

"He doesn't need to understand," William said. "His job is to bless our labors, just as your job is to terraform the planet." He pressed on Theodore's shoulder, indicating a pew closer to the altar, where waited their wives and grown children. "Just as mine is to lead."

———

THREE WEEKS LATER, surrounded by data streams from *Melanchthon*'s sensors and observers, Theodore reviewed the terraforming plans. First, find an icy asteroid of useful composition and the right size, about seventy miles across. Melli flagged three candidates observed during the ship's deceleration into the '85 system, and his team searched the sky for more. Second, rendezvous with the chosen icy asteroid and propel it into orbit over New Augsburg. Third, bombard the planet with chunks of the icy asteroid, turning the ices into gases, giving New Augsburg an atmosphere for the first time. A smile tightened Theodore's cheeks. The expedition would let New Augsburg do most of the work in the third phase. Fourth, deploy on the planet chemical factories—stripped down versions of the fabricator that turned the crew's exhalations, sewage, and garbage into food, clothing, and equipment—to optimize New Augsburg's atmosphere for terrestrial life. Fifth, seed New Augsburg with grasses, trees, insects, and animals from the embryo banks and genetic engineering labs.

Theodore stepped back from the displays and stretched. Sixth, build a house of basalt block walls, and floor-to-ceiling picture windows facing plump red '85 across a crater lake filled with paperbelly trout....

One phase at a time. He left his office for a strategy session with his team.

"CANDIDATE BETA."

Brandon had soft eyes, a narrow chin, and a shock of brown hair combed low across his forehead. Inspired by one of William's presentations, he'd joined the expedition directly out of grad school in Austin. Smart, but he lacked the experience most older crew gained from the terraforming projects begun on Mars and Venus and ongoing climate management on Earth.

Behind Brandon, the room's far wall, a video screen, showed a sunny afternoon in a zen garden. Sand raked like ripples around mottled stones made a calm contrast to Brandon's intent face. "Candidate Beta has enough of all desired volatiles. It's closest to our present location. It's the obvious choice."

Theodore glanced at a display on the side wall, full of data on the top five candidates, then shook his head. "Beta has more mass than we need, and it's further from New Augsburg than the others." Theodore hooked his thumb over his shoulder at another display, showing progress bars for ongoing surveys. Around the room, the others on the team nodded and shifted their shoulders toward him. "We will decide after we complete—"

"I thought we came here to terraform New Augsburg." Brandon's voice echoed through the room.

Theodore set his fists on his hips. "The survey *is* terraforming."

"I heard William speak on Earth. Didn't you? 'Creating a new, habitable world is our highest duty, both to God and to humankind.'"

The others in the room—among them lanky Peter and clear-skinned

Sonya, his wife—turned pensive gazes to the zen garden. One person, a young ecologist named Frederique, nodded.

"We will do that duty," Theodore said, voice firm, "by completing the icy asteroid survey, then selecting a candidate." He held his stare on Brandon until the other's chest shrank, pulling down his face. Theodore went on. "Biology sub-team, how many frozen embryos passed the first quality control check...?"

Next day, Theodore met with William one-on-one. Luxuries festooned William's office, from potted cactuses like swollen pine cones fast-grown by the biology team to a centuries-old hard copy of *The Book of Concord*. A video wall showed a clearing in a forest of oaks and birches, with New Augsburg in the sky like a gigantic moon.

After preliminary chit-chat about their families, their cramped apartments, and the proteinaceous goop extruded by the fabricators, William frowned through his beard. "I hear there's needless delay in selecting an icy asteroid."

Theodore crossed his arms. "Brandon's talking out of turn?"

"I have an open door and won't turn anyone away. He came to me yesterday and seemed very certain Beta was good enough. Is it?"

Charts and tables filled his mind's eye. Honesty compelled his reply. "Yes."

William's mouth scrunched. "I nominated you for expedition CTO because you always seemed to know what you're doing. But if we've got a good enough icy asteroid, shouldn't we go get it?" In the video wall, a red-crested woodpecker raucously laughed.

Theodore raised his palm. "Beta is larger than we need and relatively far from New Augsburg. The survey could easily find a better one."

"We want to terraform as quickly as possible. Right?"

"Yes, but...." Theodore shifted his weight to unstick his shirt from the small of his back. "If the survey takes another month, but finds a suitable candidate requiring two fewer months to transport to New Augsburg, we come out a month ahead." He swallowed. What made him so nervous? Especially with so logical an answer—

Face craggy, William shook his head. "Technically, maybe, but this isn't an engineering problem."

"Then what is it?"

"We woke people from suspan to start terraforming. A month later and we haven't started. For the sake of morale, we need to start now."

Theodore shuffled back a half-step. "Other than Brandon, morale is fine—"

"Among your team. The fine points of terraforming elude the rest of the crew. They just want to get to work. God's work, bringing life to a barren rock under a red sun. Do that for them."

"I, I didn't think of that." Theodore angled his head down. "I'll work up a flight plan to Beta and run it by Melli tomorrow."

———

IF THE CREW needed work to keep up its morale, it found plenty of labors in the next months. The journey to Beta took a few days and consumed a tiny sliver of *Melanchthon*'s ice shield, a deeply pitted cylinder five hundred yards in diameter and five hundred tall, carried from Earth as both fuel for the conversion drives and shielding against interstellar dust grains struck at $0.2\ c$.

Fusing the ice shield with Beta's bulk of frozen water, methane, and ammonia took a few days more. The deceleration burn shone blinding light, the conversion drives' exhaust, on Beta's north pole. Light bright enough to melt ices to liquid water and outgassing methane.

Melanchthon yawed 180°. A nudge from the drives and the ice shield slid into the pool of melt water. The front attitude drives arrested the ship's motion relative to Beta. The crew only needed to wait for the melt water to refreeze in the deep interplanetary cold before *Melanchthon*'s drives kicked in again.

Though the ship pushed Beta inward at the maximum acceleration the drives could safely generate, Theodore couldn't feel the thrust. The delivery to New Augsburg orbit would still take eighteen months.

In every meeting with William, Theodore quickly ran through the many tasks remaining before Beta would be ready for the bombardment phase. Teams rode three-man crawlers—cramped globes with eight articulated legs and pitons instead of feet—across Beta's surface and deployed small explosive charges and seismic arrays as they went. Tedious work, melting holes in the ice, inserting explosives and sensors, and waiting until the holes froze over before continuing their crawl. After the teams returned to the warmth and relative openness of *Melanchthon*, the geologists remotely detonated the charges and picked up transmitted data from the sensor arrays.

A week later, the geologists gave Theodore and his team a map of Beta's interior.

A month later, the geologists gave them an estimated minimum safe duration of the bombardment phase.

———

"TWENTY-THREE MONTHS?" Brandon said.

Theodore set his hands on his hips. "Are you blaming God for the tensile strength of ice?" he asked. One of his senior team members chuckled.

Brandon lifted his head and sighted down his nose. "No true member of our expedition would question what God has done, or will do. We know He has called us to terraform New Augsburg." He leaned forward and his eyes gleamed like he held a game-winning card. "I question what men will do."

"We worked out phase three before *Melanchthon* left Sol system."

"I worked out a better one." Brandon swept his shock of brown hair back from his eyes and strode to the meeting room's main display.

The display held a schematic of phase three, updated with data from the geologists. Pocked gray New Augsburg hung in the center, ringed by a concentric dashed circle about 2.4 times larger—the planet's Roche limit. A dotted line parallel to a tangent entered the dashed circle. Just barely inside, the dotted line held a green X. Lines of text next to the green X contrasted with the black, star-dusted background. *vo = 3283 m/s. r = 10608.14 km.*

Brandon stopped at the display, then turned to Theodore. He touched his hands together at the fingertips, then absently nodded to Theodore. "The original phase three was adequate. Disengage from Beta just inside the Roche limit and with not quite enough orbital velocity to maintain its altitude above New Augsburg."

He touched the display. Beta appeared at the X and the display zoomed in. "The planet's gravity does two things. First, its tidal force rips Beta apart. Second, its centripetal force spirals Beta in." On the display, Beta elongated and shed chunks, and its center of mass crept slowly inward from the dashed circle, like a car drifting away from the lane markers on a country highway.

"Because we don't want Beta to fall to New Augsburg in big pieces—too much kinetic energy might send some of our new atmosphere back into space, too much dust in our new atmosphere may reduce insolation for subsequent steps—we need to keep it in its decaying orbit long enough for the tidal force to rip it into small enough pieces. More than adequate, that's... clever."

Theodore's gaze flicked from the screen to Brandon's smug face. "It's also the best plan we have."

Brandon stared back. "We can speed up the process." He turned to the display, stopped the animation. His fingers called up a video file while he talked over his shoulder. "A geologist friend and I looked at Beta's interior map and found eight locations where sub-megaton fusion explosives could accelerate Beta's disintegration, thus allowing faster deorbiting of its fragments."

Gooseflesh swept over Theodore's arms. "Back on Earth, we called 'fusion explosives' hydrogen bombs."

"Earth is 8.31 light years away."

"We can't build hydrogen bombs—"

"Fusion explosives are feasible. The fabricator has specs for a hydrogen pelleter and implosion lasers, and Beta contains all the hydrogen we need."

"You'll neutron activate fragments of bomb casings and laser hardware. You'll litter New Augsburg with fallout."

"Scattered over the entire planet, any fallout would be nearly undetectable."

Theodore stepped back. Darn it, Brandon had a point. Hydrogen bombs would release a fraction of the energy generated by the matter-to-energy conversion drives.

Still... conversion drives served a useful purpose. Hydrogen bombs.... Sonya turned aghast eyes on Brandon. The corners of Peter's mouth curled down.

Hydrogen bombs? Handguns would use far less energy, yet none were found on *Melanchthon*. "Hydrogen bombs were a threat to all life on Earth. How can you even think this might be a good idea?"

"Is a fusion explosive good or evil? Or is men's use of it what makes it good or evil?"

Theodore's stomach churned. "The use, not the tool. But—"

"Terraforming New Augsburg is our highest purpose. The sooner we terraform it, the better." Brandon swept the others with an expression of otherworldly confidence. "All true members of our expedition agree with me."

Younger people in the room nodded. Markus, another senior team member, showed a tight face, indicating to Theodore he wrestled with Brandon's words.

Theodore put his hand up between Brandon and himself. "Your proposal has some merit, but it's a large deviation from the original plan. I have to discuss it with William before I can agree to it."

Up flexed the corners of Brandon's mouth. "Do what you must."

———

WILLIAM SAT with his feet on his desk. He rotated in his broad hands a model of *Melanchthon*, built out of plastic slivers and modeling cement by a crewman and given to him as a gift, while Theodore spoke. "...technically, it's feasible, but it's a major change of plan."

The model fixed into position. Bright mirrors, the parabolic reflectors of the conversion drives, dazzled Theodore's eyes. "If it's technically feasible," William said, "and covers New Augsburg with an atmosphere faster, why resist it?"

"Why resist hydrogen bombs? Imagine the PR nightmare on Earth."

"There's no need to tell Earth. In the seventeen years the board of directors would take to tell us no, we'll have a growing biosphere."

"So you know the board would oppose it."

William tossed the model onto his desk and swung his feet to the floor. He stood, taller than Theodore, and said, "Melli, switch the video wall to a live feed from the hull cameras."

"Which one?" the ship's feminine voice asked.

"Doesn't matter."

In Theodore's peripheral vision, the display glow reflecting off the sidewalls visibly darkened. William moved like an iceberg, massive but quiet, around his desk. He laid his hand on Theodore's shoulder and turned him toward the display.

Black space and Beta's limb of dirty snowball gray, barely lit by the field of pinpoint stars like bright dust. The stars wheeled by from *Melanchthon's* rotation.

"The board of directors is safe on Earth. Sunlight, fresh air, a community. Look what we have." His voice deepened. "Look." His broad hand pressed harder on Theodore's shoulder. "A thin skin of nanotube alloy between us and hard vacuum. Help would take eight years to learn we were in trouble and four decades after that to come to our aid. The board can't comprehend our position. We needn't bind ourselves to what we think it prefers. I'm pleased the younger people are starting to see through that. We should learn from them."

William's hand weighed on Theodore's shoulder. "You authorize hydrogen bombs."

A chuckle answered, followed by a friendly slap on the back. "No, I authorize, what did Brandon call them? 'Fusion explosives.'" William's grin melted into his beard. "Go make them work."

———

THEODORE SPENT the rest of the week, Saturday included, poring over Brandon's plan. Every challenge he raised—fabricator cycles and energy costs to build the bombs, effort and risk to deploy them—Brandon deflected with facts, figures, and youthful confidence. With the hydrogen bombs, four months to deorbit Beta in small enough chunks. Over a year and a half faster than the original plan.

Weary, late Saturday afternoon, Theodore entered the request for tunnelers and bomb construction equipment to the fabricator queue for delivery Monday morning. He watched Brandon's back until the latter walked up *Melanchthon's* curve out of sight, then went home to unwind.

Unwinding eluded him, despite the warm smells of protein schnitzel and red cabbage-flavored fiber strands. Family dinner with his wife, Helen, his daughter, Alexandra the doctor, still in scrubs from her shift, and his son-in-law, Daniel, soon devolved into bickering between Helen and Alexandra.

"We won't be at home in this star system until we start having children," Helen said.

Alexandra dropped her fork, leaned back, folded her arms. In the cramped apartment, her elbows brushed Daniel and the video wall. "It's still about finally becoming a grandma, huh?"

Helen gasped. Theodore scowled. "Your mother is an early childhood education specialist without children to educate—"

"Dad—"

"Hey, everyone, why argue?" Daniel spoke next. The rejuvenation treatments provided to all crew made him look a decade younger than his age of thirty-four. "William asked the crew to practice family planning until after we can walk on New Augsburg and breathe its air. Lexa and I will have kids after Ted makes a biosphere. Which I hear will happen faster than the original plan," he added to Theodore, then raised his beer mug.

"How?" Alexandra asked.

Daniel quirked his eyebrow and gestured at Theodore, *you answer.* Politeness or mockery?

Theodore cleared his throat. "Hy—fusion explosives."

Helen's eyes widened. "Do you mean, hydrogen bombs?"

"You can call them that."

She knitted her brows, then nodded. "I'm glad to hear you can use swords as plowshares."

For the first time in days, calm touched him. Helen never cared to know the details of his work, but she trusted that he knew them. Three awake decades together and her trust remained constant.

"It won't irradiate the material for the new atmosphere?" Alexandra asked. An honest question, based on her tone of voice, and not some effort to stir up tension.

"Not enough to worry about."

"I didn't need to ask, did I, Dad?" She smiled at him, then leaned against Daniel. "I'm glad to hear we can walk on New Augsburg sooner than the original plan." She smiled at Helen, and Daniel put his arm around her shoulders.

Theodore relaxed. His misgivings about the hydrogen bombs retreated from the bright circle of his consciousness. Finally, family harmony on a Saturday night.

———

NEXT MORNING, the crew crowded the chapel. William and his family sat alone on the front pew, Theodore, Helen, Alexandra, and Daniel sat in the pew behind William. Brandon held hands with Frederique the ecologist, near a geologist named Carl and others.

The last chords of *A Mighty Fortress is Our God* roared out of the speakers and echoed off the stained glass on the walls. Jonas rose from his ornate, high-backed chair next to George, the junior priest, and paced to the lectern. His deep-set eyes peered down his long nose at Theodore, then he glanced at his notes and spoke.

"Deuteronomy, chapter 34, records that 'the Lord said unto Moses, This is the land which I swore unto Abraham, unto Isaac, and unto Jacob, saying, I will give it unto thy seed: I have caused thee to see it with thine eyes, but thou shalt not go over thither.'

"What was Moses' response? All we know is 'Moses the servant of the Lord died there in the land of Moab,' suggesting he died content.

"Can we imagine that? After leading his people forty years through wilderness, and not merely harsh landscapes but also a wilderness of the soul, a wilderness brought on by their own stiff-necked idolatry, Moses died at the cusp of achieving what we 'true members' of our expedition might call his 'highest purpose.'" His righteous tone made the scare quotes clear.

Mutterings trickled through the congregation, centered on Brandon. Behind the altar, in the junior pastor's chair, George scowled at Jonas' back. William stretched his arm along the hardwood pew back and slowly drummed his fingers.

Jonas peered again at Theodore. "But Moses served a higher purpose than leading his people to the Promised Land. He served the will of the Lord."

Pressure tightened Theodore's belly. He squirmed in his seat, unable to evade Jonas' piercing gaze.

The hydrogen bombs weren't my idea—

"—He heeded God's commandments when no one else, not even the first high priest, remained steadfast—"

Sweat trickled down Theodore's nape. Finally, Jonas looked away, and Theodore's breath escaped.

After the service, William strode up the center aisle without a glance at Jonas, or Theodore. For the best, for his eyes held cold fury. Brandon held back until William strode by, then led his cluster of young crew out of the pew.

Theodore trudged up the aisle, Helen's hand on his arm and her brow crinkled. Three times muscles flowed in her face as if she would speak, but not until they pushed through the doors into the narthex did she speak. "What's the matter, honey?"

"I—" He cleared his throat. "I need to speak to Jonas."

"I'll wait with—" Normally, after a Sunday service, the narthex held dozens of people, serving as a fellowship hall in *Melanchthon*'s tight layout. Now, only about fifteen people remained in inner-directed clumps of two or three. "Where is everyone?"

Words came to Theodore's mind, along with an odd feeling weighing down on him. Suddenly it seemed important to murmur the words just to her. "Many people disliked Jonas' sermon."

"Why would someone dislike his sermon?" she said, too loud.

Theodore sucked in a breath and his eyes widened. He lifted his hand enough to wave his fingers, *quiet*.

"Why indeed?" came Jonas' voice from behind Theodore. The senior pastor stood in a long white robe like a pillar of smoke. Another robed figure, the junior pastor, George, grunted a civil farewell at Jonas and walked on.

"Dear, I'll be a moment with Jonas." Theodore beckoned toward the far corner of the narthex. A wall sconce softly lit a small round table holding a Bible and a vase of plastic lilies. Jonas walked with him, peering sidelong until Theodore touched his elbow and squared shoulders to him.

"The hydrogen bombs weren't my idea," he said.

Unblinking, Jonas said, "They weren't?"

"One of my subordinates pushed them."

"Brandon?"

"He's got William's ear. Between the two of them, I couldn't refuse."

Jonas turned to the small round table, flipped open the Bible. His finger tracked down a page, then swept under a line. Sarcasm filled his next words. "'I am innocent of the blood of this just person: see ye to it.'"

The page heading showed Matthew 27. Theodore's gaze stuck to a name near Jonas' finger.

Theodore's neck turned clammy. "I'm not like Pilate."

"A truly innocent man lacks any urge to proclaim his innocence." Jonas' deep eyes were like the muzzles of high-caliber pistols. "You've unleashed on New Augsburg a monstrosity better left in Sol system. You cannot wash your hands of it."

Jonas trickled his finger down the page, then turned and paced away on his narrow feet.

Every eye in the narthex stared at Theodore. He shifted his weight away from them, his back seeking the wall... but two of the eyes belonged to Helen. She came closer, her eyes and the set of her mouth full of trust and love.

On top of that, if Jonas was now his enemy, William and Brandon were now his allies.

———

SEVENTEEN MONTHS REMAINED to slowly propel Beta inside New Augsburg's Roche limit. Not much time for a crew of a hundred fifty to modify phase three.

The eight fusion explosive sites each lay miles under Beta's dusty ice surface. Three-man crews in tunnelers—vehicles ringed with piton legs around their midsections, giant roller drill bits for noses, and heat vents in their tails—chewed through Beta at a crawl, two yards per minute. Theodore put on a transcranial stim helmet and entered a virtual of a tunneler crew compartment to see just how hard the crews worked. A hot and sweaty space the size of a small car's interior, the drill bits constantly roaring on Beta's ice, tailings banging and scraping over the tunneler's hull toward the tail. Flashes of heat from the vents vaporized some tailings, and like a gun, propelled more up the tunnel toward the surface. Given the hundreds of miles of tunnels drilled through Beta, crews stayed in the tunnelers for ten days at a time.

Nine months after the acceleration started, with '85 still a dim red point two billion miles away, *Melanchthon* started its deceleration burn. Not an easy task; the ship's attitude drives couldn't swing Beta's peta-tons of ices. After acceleration cut out, Melli and the crew worked together to aim *Melanchthon*'s forward retrodrives to melt a circle around the part of the rotating coupling frame buried in Beta. A day's burn later, the coupling frame burst free of the melt water pond. Spilling drops froze into ice pellets and lacquered the coupling frame with hard rime.

Flying around Beta, melting water at its south pole with the main drives in the stern, and inserting the coupling frame took three days more.

The tunneler crews kept working after the deceleration burn started. Their journeys to and from *Melanchthon* took even longer now, four hours in a surface crawler from the ship to the nearest mouth of the tunnel system. The south polar mouth of the tunnels lay eight miles from *Melanchthon*, a safety precaution for the fusion detonations. The explosions would vaporize cubic kilometers of ices, and the resulting steam would vent out of the tunnel system like a tail outgassing from a sun-warmed comet. With the tunnel mouth distant, the steam would jet well clear of *Melanchthon*'s position.

Meanwhile, on an upper deck near the ship's axis, separators received a constant stream of ice gouged out of Beta and sent chilled hydrogen to the pelleter. Though the other materials were fed to *Melanchthon*'s fabricators through impermeable piping, the stink of ammonia tinged the air all the way down on the outermost deck. Magnets held half-assembled bombs and laser implosion assemblies on the outside of the hull near the spin axis, under the rotating coupling between *Melanchthon* and Beta. They waited, inert, as the tunnelers progressed and '85 enlarged into a dull red disc visible through the hull's rearward cameras.

A small white dot, at first glance a star, resolved into a crescent. In another virtual, Theodore's heart rocked his entire body. New Augsburg as he would see it with his physical eyes, if he could stand on the hull amid glaring luminous drive exhausts and breath hard vacuum. New Augsburg, soon to be their home.

If the fusion explosives made New Augsburg livable sooner, they were worth Jonas' disapproval.

———

THE DAY SOON CAME. New Augsburg looked as large as a soccer ball held a foot from one's eyes. Long shadows near the terminator showed the planet's surface roughness. A wild terrain, full of gorgeous views, of mountains and hills, of crater lakes and eternal sunrises....

Theodore shut his eyes and took a refocusing breath. He sat in *Melanchthon*'s chapel, along with a hundred crew members. Expectation filled the room. The conversion drives' labor, at full power for a year and a half, brought the ship and Beta to New Augsburg's Roche limit with a velocity too low for Beta to remain in orbit. Separate the two halves of the rotating coupling, detonate the fusion explosives armed and deployed inside the tunnel system, and within two months, Beta would become New Augsburg's atmosphere and hydrosphere.

On the chapel's front wall, the video displays remained in position below and to the sides of the cross. The left-hand display showed the view from the bow cameras, where Beta's dirty white bulk and the coupling frame wheeled around. In the display to the right, New Augsburg hung in space, an inert rock soon, through God's will and the crew's hands, brought to life.

He reached for Helen's hand. She took his and squeezed.

Melli's voice came through the speakers. "Roche limit reached. Velocity below orbital velocity. All systems check green."

In the front pew, William stood up. Crowd noise faded away. "Melli, decouple from Beta."

"Decoupling from Beta." If all went well, explosive bolts would separate the halves of the rotating coupling and push *Melanchthon* away from Beta at 5 m/s.

He lurched forward, like hitting the brakes on a car. He squeezed Helen's hand. "We're clear."

Cheers and applause echoed through the chapel. On the left display, a tetrad of nanotube-alloy arms—the coupling frame—left behind on Beta's surface receded from view.

"Decoupling complete," Melli said.

"Good." William's voice filled the chapel. The crowd again silenced itself. "Spin us around and prepare for reorbit burn."

"Rotating 180°." A brief sideways shudder, then only the ship's spin gravity. The coupling frame slid to the left and off-screen. The rest of Beta slowly followed.

"Switch left display to stern camera view," William said.

The display switched. A dull white arc crept onto the display from the right edge. Eventually, the coupling frame, looking a third as large as it had before, came into view. Another shudder of the ship and the coupling frame locked into position, wheeling around the center of the display, shrinking with each moment.

"All systems check green for reorbit burn."

"Detonate the fusion explosives, then commence burn."

"Detonating fusion explosives."

Theodore held his breath. Beta continued to wheel in the left display. The icy asteroid's surface lacked any sign of the intense energies unleashed within it. Vaporizing ices, propagating cracks, fracturing Beta into dozens of smaller particles.

"Commencing burn one meter-per-second-squared, delta vee plus sixty meters-per-second," Melli said. Acceleration nudged Theodore, Helen, and the others against the pew backs. The conversion drives pulsed into a seamless net thrust.

On the display, the coupling frame shrank even faster from view. A fuzzy mass of whiter ice marked melted and refrozen tailings on Beta's surface around the tunnel mouth, four miles away from the coupling frame. The jet should look spectac—

The coupling frame. Suddenly larger. Ice around it cracking like an eggshell. Wisps of hot gas boiling around them. The coupling frame and a jagged chunk of ice carried with it now filling the display.

Theodore's blood ran cold. "No."

Helen tightened her grip on his hand. A few gasps sounded in the chapel.

"Terminating burn," Melli said, synthetic feminine voice far too calm.

The coupling frame collided with *Melanchthon*'s stern. Theodore tumbled sideways into Helen. William fell, jutting out his hands. Throughout the chapel, people clutched at pew backs and one another's hands. Something heavy smacked wood.

William rose to one knee. Brandon, along with Carl the geologist, ran forward and offered their hands. He waved them off and clambered to his feet. "Melli, what happened?"

On the left display, the coupling frame and its chunk of ice, still spinning, tumbled slowly away from *Melanchthon*'s stern camera. Behind them, a pillar of fire lanced out of the tunnel mouth. Cracks raced across Beta's surface.

Theodore gulped. *We didn't map Beta's fault lines well enough.*

"The vapor front generated by the fusion explosives apparently took an unexpected path toward the surface, which propelled a mass of ice with the coupling frame embedded with sufficient velocity to collide with *Melanchthon*."

A sudden hubbub came from halfway up the center aisle. William's voice thundered. "How did this happen?"

Melli spoke in a matter-of-fact tone. "Our analysis of Beta's interior may have been incomplete—"

"My gosh, he's hurt!" called a woman's voice from the middle of the chapel. "Alexandra, quick!"

Theodore and Helen craned their necks. Alexandra slipped out of the pew past her husband and Frederique. Features tight, she sprinted up the aisle. Theodore stood. A fabricator tech lay on the beige carpet, his head near the solid birch pew. Eyes glassy, he twitched, and blood seeped from his temple. Alexandra knelt, pressed her fingers to his neck. Her mouth tightened and she looked to the ceiling. "Melli, send a robot gurney, stat."

"The robot gurneys are all en route to other injured crew members."

Alexandra's mouth compressed. "All four of them? Unless everyone else has a head injury, get one here. Now!"

Spots swam in Theodore's vision. He slumped into the pew and his head sank to his hands. His stomach turned queasy.

Breathe. *Melanchthon* survived. Five crew members hurt, but Alexandra and the medical robots would heal them. Breathe.

At least the hydrogen bombs weren't your idea—

Jonas' deep-set, disapproving stare filled his mind's eye.

Theodore inhaled deeply. Jonas had been right. Approving Brandon's plan made him responsible for the injuries and any damage *Melanchthon* suffered, no less than Brandon.

Or William.

———

BLEARY from a late night with his team, reviewing Beta's seismic map and checking diagnostics on the animal embryo storage tanks, followed by five hours of restless sleep, Theodore approached William's office. An assistant, a young man with a round face and soft voice, put a caller on hold and, over the ping of incoming messages on his tablet, bade Theodore wait in the anteroom.

How long had William had an assistant? A temporary measure, dealing with yesterday's near disaster, most likely. Theodore shuffled his feet and studied a 3d-printed statuette of Vikings players lifting the Lombardi Trophy fifty years earlier. Oh, to relax and watch a football game for a few hours—

"He'll see you now," the assistant said.

Inside his office, William stood beside new furniture—a round, walnut-brown table and two chairs—near the video wall. New Augsburg hung over the clearing in the north woods. Beta, too, hung in the sky, cracked into twenty pieces, each piece shedding ice particles from the ends nearest and furthest from New Augsburg. A live camera shot.

At least the fusion explosives did their job.

"Have a seat," William said. His beard trimmed and edged, his long-sleeved button-front shirt clean and pressed—he looked far more alert than Theodore felt.

Theodore came forward, gaze on William's face. Hooded eyes, what did they mean, and scraping his upper teeth over the beard on his lower lip? Theodore sat and William did the same.

"Rumor has it the ship is undamaged and the injured crew will heal," Theodore said. "That's true?"

"True. The collision bent one drive reflector. The rest of the drives will keep us in orbit until Melli and a repair crew fix it. We might not even need a repair. *Melanchthon* will never leave '85's system, after all."

A question formed behind Theodore's face. William answered it. "Six injuries. Four broken limbs, two skull fractures. Alexandra expects full recoveries from everyone, including the head injuries. Be proud of your daughter."

Some of his unease melted away. "I am."

William gazed at the tabletop. His large hand slowly spiraled across uneven patches in the walnut brown stain. Odd to order an intentionally imperfect table from the fabricators. "Either we got lucky or God watched out for us. Enough of the vaporized gases from inside Beta vented out the main tunnel to reduce the collision speed of the coupling frame. Kinetic energy, vee-squared something, right?"

The complete equation sprang to Theodore's mind. An irrelevancy, he set it aside. "What might have happened without tunnel venting?" he asked quietly.

"Melli ran some plausible numbers. A hull breach, for one. Even worse—"

"Worse? Than a hull breach?"

William's hand stopped moving. "Loss of containment of the exotic matter catalyst in a conversion drive. The catalyst would drift through the ship, triggering enough uncontrolled conversion of matter to energy to blow *Melanchthon* to pieces."

Theodore slumped in his seat. The expedition could have died, when he could have saved it. "I didn't protest the hydrogen bombs enough. Brandon wanted them, you wanted them—"

"The fusion explosives were not the problem," William said. "We missed something in the interaction between the detonations and Beta's structure. Right? Site them differently, put in more venting, something would have kept *Melanchthon* safe."

Pieces of the problem flew through Theodore's mind, collided, drifted apart. "Get further from Beta before detonating."

"Something." William shrugged. "We need to find out what. Not for our sake, we're done delivering icy asteroids to New Augsburg. But for every other terraforming expedition Earth might send out."

Every other expedition which, whether couched in spiritual terms or not, did God's work by spreading life to empty star systems. "I agree."

"Good. And who would be better for the job than you and your senior team members?"

"No one." His subconscious sifted dossiers.

"Exactly. Start now. Be thorough, then be quick. There's a lot of data to review from the geologists, the demolition teams siting the fusion explosives, *Melanchthon*'s specs... I want weekly updates and a final report before Beta's fragments strike New Augsburg."

Two months. Theodore licked his lips, nodded. "We'll do that."

"You look doubtful."

"No, no, it's just a lot of work to add to our stack. Fine-tuning the atmosphere processors—"

"Be a leader. Delegate. Hand the routine matters to Brandon."

"Brandon?"

"Yes, Brandon." William narrowed his eyes. "You have a problem with him?"

"He proposed the hydrogen bombs—"

"No one foresaw the accident. Not him. Not you. He has a lot of zeal to complete the project as soon as possible. You can't think that's a problem, can you?"

Again, Theodore licked his lips. "No, but—"

"The atmosphere processors can't explode. There's no harm in handing off phase four to him." William leaned forward. "Is there?"

Cool wet stuck Theodore's shirt to the small of his back. He shifted against his chair's backrest and said, "Of course not."

———

NEXT SUNDAY, the junior pastor, George, led the service. He did all the right things—singing along with *A Mighty Fortress is Our God*, leading a prayer for the two crew members in the infirmary with skull fractures, asking God's blessing on Theodore's investigation of the accident, as well as on Brandon's direction of phase four. His sermon quoted 2 Corinthians 4: Troubled on every side, yet not distressed; perplexed, but not in despair. The crew did God's work, terraforming New Augsburg as rapidly as possible.

George did all the right things, while Jonas sat behind the altar in the senior pastor's chair, his deep-set gaze flicking from George to William.

Theodore shuddered. Jonas too faced an ambitious subordinate encouraged by the expedition's CEO.

———

"I TELL YOU, the data analysis is incomplete, and Melli's simulation runs of the explosions are not reproducible." Theodore drew a breath, deepened his voice. "My team's only certain conclusion is *Melanchthon* should have moved further from Beta before detonating the hydrogen bombs."

William said nothing, then lifted a glass of whiskey from the tabletop. Light from the video wall, New Augsburg and fragmenting Beta hanging over the forest clearing, danced in the brown liquid. "That will not be the only comment in your final report." He sipped. His unperturbed face suggested the fabricators made a very smooth whiskey... or he drank more frequently than one glass during his last meeting on a Friday afternoon.

"That's where the facts point. The facts matter, don't they? Not for us, but for other terraforming expeditions?"

The whiskey glass' thick base thunked on the tabletop. "Of course facts matter. But you think the only facts relate to mass and energy? No." He circled his hand in the air, indicating the entire crew. "Psychological facts matter at least as much."

Theodore folded his arms. "How?"

William reached for the whiskey glass, then nudged it away. "Let's say we made a mistake and detonated too soon after separation."

"I just did."

"Your team's report won't go just from the filesystem to Earth. Copies will remain on board indefinitely. Copies crew members might read."

The board of directors insisted on data transparency during the expedition's planning stages. Documents published by the expedition would be available to all crew. "And?"

"And what might someone conclude? The expedition might have been destroyed because Brandon, me, and you authorized premature detonation?"

"We made a mistake. People will forgive that."

"No. They'll say they forgive it, but underneath, they'll doubt everything we do. 'Do the terraformers need all those fabricator cycles? How many atmosphere processors do they need?' Later, they'll ask why the ecologists released so many—" He rolled his wrists in a shrug. "—wolves, snakes, ticks, bacteria, whatever."

He sipped more whiskey. "If they doubt us, they may not follow us. Terraforming will face a lot of challenges where they should follow us."

Like charges seeking ground, aborted impulses to speak jolted partway down Theodore's arms, partway to his vocal cords. Most crew didn't understand the terraformers' work, but how could it serve God's will to hide the truth? "You want me to lie?"

"Theodore." William spoke like a parent frustrated at a child bringing home report card Bs. "Mention premature detonation in your report, that's fine. But make sure you describe other factors that might have contributed to the accident. If you lack the data to conclude which factor contributed the most, then lead with that lack of data as the single biggest factor. Not hard at all."

Not hard, except during the next months, William requested edits and more work on draft after draft. More simulation runs, more data analysis, more speculation about what data would have enabled an accurate model of Beta's interior.

Theodore drafted new text while sitting in the chapel pew, with the crew cheering the video display of Beta's fragments impacting New Augsburg's sunlit face. Theodore reviewed simulation runs in his office with the door half closed, while Brandon led a team meeting about deployment of the atmosphere processors. Theodore scrolled through William's latest edits on his tablet while rounding the last corner before the men's room.

"Whoa! Pardon me, I'm sorry, sir." The fabricator tech, fully recovered except for a faint scar on his temple, smelling faintly of solvents and sintered plastic.

"Quite all right."

"No, no, we're here to help the terraformers. That's what Pastor George said. I should watch where I'm going when you're busy working." The tech wiped his hands on his jeans' threadbare thighs.

"Don't worry about it." The tech lifted his hands. Theodore frowned at the fraying denim.

"Oh, sir, don't worry, I won't jump the queue for new jeans. I know you need fab cycles for atmosphere processors, and animal exogestators after that. I'll wait my turn, sir."

What had Brandon done while the accident report dominated Theodore's time? "Don't wait so long your jeans fray into cutoffs."

The tech laughed. "Thank you, sir, but I'd wear rags every day if it helped the terraformers bring life faster to New Augsburg."

THANKS TO BETA, New Augsburg now had an atmosphere, and thanks to '85, a planet-wide convection cell driving the atmosphere's circulation. The atmosphere was thick enough—thirty-two PSI, eighty percent of it nitrogen—that nitrogen, oxygen, and carbon dioxide would remain gaseous, even in the perpetual cold of the dark side. Water vapor would fall on the dark side as snow, forming glaciers. *Melanchthon* dipped into the upper atmosphere, using its conversion drive exhaust to sculpt rivers from the glaciers across the habitable zone to evaporate under '85's incessant rays.

The convection cell meant a cold wind would continually blow from darkward across the habitable zone. A cold wind at Theodore's back when he went down to the crater lake to fish, warmed by the habitable zone's eternal sunrise.

A thick enough atmosphere, yet it contained only molecules born from lifeless chemistry, without the free oxygen terrestrial life needed.

Hence the atmosphere processors. Stripped-down, custom-built fabricators, with broad solar panels powering a handful of gas purifications and chemical reactions. Split oxygen from water vapor and carbon dioxide, with residual carbon and hydrogen turned into carbohydrates to feed living things. Extract ammonia from the air for use as fertilizer. Catalyze alkane chain extension, turning gaseous methane into liquid hexane pumped into gas-tight bladders.

After William tightbeamed the final draft of his report on the Beta incident to Earth, Theodore reviewed the atmosphere processors' specs and drawings. Bodies the size and shape of shipping containers on self-leveling legs, with solar panels on the roof ready to pop up and orient toward '85 like black rectangular flowers. Automated gliders, deployed during the river-sculpting runs, would carry them to the sunlit faces of hilltops near the terminator. Despite Brandon's taking charge of phase four, the specs remained unchanged from the originals drawn up on Earth.

The number of processors, though, had doubled, at Brandon's request. Double the number of processors, cut the duration of phase four in half, from ten months to five until human beings could walk the planet's surface and breath its air. Theodore's teeth ground. Brandon need only have said *We came here to terraform New Augsburg* with idealistic fire in his voice and hints of William's approval trailing him, and the fab manager would have yielded.

Just like you yielded, recurred a thought, over and over when Theodore stared at the dim nanotube alloy ceiling, Helen's forearm and knee brushing him in the narrow bed as she dozed, unaware of his sleeplessness.

———

THEY CALLED IT REFORMATION CITY. A hundred shelters as squared-off and cramped as their shipboard apartments, each set on a two-acre lot seeded with green-black geneteched bermudagrass. A fabricator, a biergarten, a clinic, a school, and a town hall. The campus for the terraforming department, labs and greenhouses, animal exogestators and robot maintenance sheds. A boxy, double-height church, laid out inside like the ship's chapel, except for windows between the altar and the cross admitting the red light of '85, illumining the top of the rear wall.

The public buildings of the town occupied a gray-palette tableland, product of thawed and resolidified lava from a sculpting run, on the bank of a river they named the Schlosskirche. A pumping station at the river watered the town and a cell tower on the tableland allowed its inhabitants to talk to one another when *Melanchthon* was below the horizon. The shelters spilled down over the lowlands away from the river, mostly straddling a dirt track running eight miles to the landing field for *Melanchthon*'s shuttles. Seven miles beyond the landing field, the nearest atmosphere processor showed as a dark spot on a hilltop. *Melanchthon*, orbiting on autopilot, zipped overhead every eighty minutes.

A far cry from picture windows overlooking a crater lake, but that would come in time, after the ecologists seeded a biosphere circling the planet.

Once the last of the crew landed, the pastor held a convocation at eight o'clock the next morning. In the never-ending sunrise of '85, the twenty-four-hour ship's clock was arbitrary, as were concepts of morning and night; but circadian rhythms cycled in human brains, and the fabricators had provided Sol-spectrum lamps and blackout curtains for each shelter and public building. Theodore and Helen walked upslope ten minutes before the hour, up a path along a rock track scraped of surface dust, gulping thick air, holding hands. He walked on the path's darkward side, partially shielding his wife from the cold wind. '85 hung behind her head like a red halo. The morning seemed it could last forever.

They reached the church five minutes early. William and his wife climbed out of a blocky off-road vehicle with knobby tires and bulging with battery packs.

William wrapped his broad hand around Theodore's. "Good to see you."

A distracted nod, then Theodore said, "When did you get—" He lifted his chin toward the off-roader. '85's reflection sheened in silver metallic paint on the quarterpanel. "—that?"

"The fab team parked it in our driveway and coded it to our biometrics before we landed. I'll give you a spin later." His wide hand pressed on Theodore's shoulder. "Time to get inside."

William and his wife took the front pew. Brandon, Frederique, Carl, Alexandra, and Daniel already occupied the second pew. Theodore and Helen squeezed in next to their son-in-law.

The church service began like the ones on the ship. The speakers poured out the chords of *A Mighty Fortress is Our God*, augmented by a hundred and fifty imperfect but enthusiastic voices. Prayers and scripture readings. George gave the first homily on Joshua. Thus far, the terraformers had, in effect, spied on the Canaanites. Seeding the biosphere would topple the walls of Jericho, under a sun standing still as at Gibeon.

When George left the lectern and Jonas gathered himself up from the senior pastor's chair, a frown creased Theodore's brow. He pulled a tablet preloaded with a Bible app and swiped forward to Joshua 13, where Joshua divided the promised land among the tribes by lot.

He glanced at the back of William's thick neck and shivered.

Jonas took the lectern. His homily began with a parallel between the crew and David's thirty-seven mighty men, of whom he mentioned four by name—a flicker narrowed Theodore's eyes at only name, Uriah the Hittite.

He hit the Bible app's search box as Jonas went on. Courageous men, serving a king whom they believed to be just.

Theodore found 2 Samuel 11. Jonas' tone darkened. A king who abducted and impregnated Uriah's wife, and ordered Uriah's abandonment on the battlefield.

William lifted his arm to the pew back. His fingers drummed the fabbed wood at a funereal pace.

"And the prophet Nathan told David, that the sword would never leave his house. And so it happened. A son's insurrection against his father. A kingdom divided. A weak king overmastered by his pagan wife. Invasion inflicted on the land."

William's fingers drummed faster.

Jonas slowly shook his head, then settled his gaze on William. "As the prophet Micah tells us, in the second chapter of his book: 'Woe to them that devise iniquity, and work evil upon their beds! when the morning is light, they practise it, because it is in the power of their hand. And they covet fields, and take them by violence; and houses, and take them away: so they oppress a man and his house, even a man and his heritage. Therefore thus saith the Lord; Behold, against this family do I devise an evil....'"

The drumming fingers stopped. William's hand wrapped the top of the pew back. He pushed himself to his feet, then gripped his wife's elbow and guided her up, her profile showing puzzlement fading to submission. His gaze swept across the second pew, from Theodore across to Brandon. William led his wife up the center aisle, toward the rear wall bathed in '85's red light. In his wake, the congregation bubbled like a pot coming to boil.

Jonas' voice thundered from the speakers. "'And I said, Hear, I pray you, O heads of Jacob, and ye princes of the house of Israel; Is it not for you to know judgment? Who hate the good, and love the evil; who pluck off their skin from off them, and their flesh from off their bones; Who also eat the flesh of my people, and flay their skin from off them; and they break their bones, and chop them in pieces, as for the pot, and as flesh within the caldron.'"

The thud of the sanctuary doors closing behind William answered.

Brandon stood. Frederique, Carl, Daniel, joined him. Alexandra too, her quirked eyebrow questioning Theodore. Brandon slipped out the far side of the pew, passing in front of stained glass showing a Sanhedrin officer striking Christ with his hand. His girlfriend and friends soon followed him up the side aisle toward the exit.

Alexandra gave Theodore an imploring look, until Daniel tugged her hand. She shuffled away, pulling part of Theodore's heart with her.

He turned his heavy head toward the lectern. A flame burned in Jonas' face, blue-white, hot enough to distill gold from crushed rock. Jonas' expression could only burn the impure. Theodore locked his gaze on Jonas like solar panels deployed toward '85 and accepted his discomfort.

George, the junior pastor, rose from his chair. He strode between the lectern and the altar and up the center aisle.

———

SUMMONED the next day to William's office, Theodore arrived five minutes early. The assistant offered water and coffee and asked him to wait, just a few minutes. Theodore sat on a chair with smooth wooden arms and plush cushions, under a fabbed reproduction of a Rembrandt. Half an hour later, and ten minutes after George left William's office without a glance at Theodore, the assistant bade him enter.

The faint stink of cured construction adhesive touched Theodore's nose. William's office filled one end of the third and highest story of the town hall. Floor-to-ceiling windows gave a panoramic view over the church, where '85 hung below the top of the belfry, over the Schlosskirche River and jumbled gray plains beyond the far bank, to deepening dark behind William's desk to the right. Just over the terminator, jagged red dots marked a crater rim's wall poking its summits into sunlight. A classical symphony, Haydn or early Mozart, cantered from hidden speakers.

"Pause music. Theodore, take a seat." William gestured at a clubby chair upholstered in thick brown leather facing the desk. Despite Theodore's unease, his body wanted to sink into the cushion. The most comfortable chair on the planet, except for the one behind the desk that William now occupied. The expedition CEO rocked his chair and scraped his upper teeth through his beard, faint sounds in the now silent room.

After a time, William said, "You disappointed me yesterday."

"How?"

"How? I know you pretend to be beyond politics, you just want to terraform, but don't act dumb. Jonas stirred up disgruntlement from the pulpit. I didn't accept it. Many younger crew members didn't accept it. Heck, even George the junior priest didn't accept it. But you did."

Theodore wavered, then sat taller. "Walking out of a service strikes me as rude."

"I'm rude?" William's face seemed an armored mask.

Theodore took a breath. "Did he hit home?"

The armored mask hardened even more. "You think I'm some evil king of ancient Israel?"

"Do you? There's a proverb, 'The wicked flee when no man pursueth.'"

William shrank back in his chair.

Theodore leaned forward. The model of *Melanchthon* on a display shelf caught one corner of his eye, and a decanter of whiskey on a small table near the window, the other. "How much throughput has the fab spent on your luxuries? An office bigger than a family's shelter, full of status marking trinkets. The only off-road vehicle reserved for personal use. You groom the young people needed to seed a biosphere, and the young priest needed to tell the rest of the crew your riches are God's plan. You're not the friend I knew back on Earth, when New Augsburg was only a dream and you needed wealthy donors—and skilled terraformers—" William's friendship always had been false. The realization poured ice water into Theodore's gut. "—to make it a reality. Change your ways, now. For the sake of our billion descendants who might live out there." He flung his arm toward the windows facing the Schlosskirche and the gray rockscape beyond.

"I'm not the friend you knew on Earth? You aren't mine."

Theodore's arm dropped. What?

William ambled to the small table, pulled the decanter cork with a *thwoom*. He poured one glass, then faced the darkward window and sipped. "You had a vision, once. The original phase three seemed so bold when you sketched it out on the whiteboard at Society headquarters. But then you stopped having vision and coasted on your past laurels. And when someone comes along with vision...."

"Brandon? He's a reckless boy—"

"He's our new chief terraforming officer."

Theodore sagged into his seat, clutching his gut. Brandon, William, no.... "The senior team members won't take his orders."

"Brandon, Carl, and Frederique won't take yours. You want to protect your status more than you want to terraform New Augsburg. They know that and they'll tell every older team member that. Your older team members are less loyal to you than you think. On top of that, our new senior paster, George, might dust off Jonas' homily yesterday to condemn you."

"You, you wouldn't."

A shrug of William's broad upper back, a sip from the glass palmed in his thick hand. "Reformation City is a small town. We capped the expedition at a hundred fifty members so everyone could know everyone else. That means rumor. Gossip. Little privacy and fewer secrets."

He turned then. A smile distended his beard yet his eyes remained cool. "You can remain active. We'll name you Emeritus CTO, freeing you from day-to-day management to consult on the big picture." William yanked open a drawer of the table and pulled out a glass. His hand throttled the decanter's neck. "Let's drink to that."

Emeritus. A fancy word for retired. "No."

William's eyes narrowed. "Too early in the morning for you, you must mean. You can't be turning down my offer."

"I can't?"

"Salvage what's left to you." William's face twisted and he plunked the unopened decanter back on the tabletop. "Who prioritizes the Reformation City fabricator? Who schedules the teams that will construct honest-to-God houses? Who runs the longevity clinic? Not you. If you want your house and fishing pier on a crater lake and time enough to enjoy them, an Emeritus CTO who helped envision New Augsburg would have earned them. But a man who lost his team's confidence?" William shook his head.

Theodore slumped in his chair. He looked past William, to the reddened tips of dark side mountains under coldly glittering stars. *You can't win. Salvage what's left.*

"I'll—" His voice cracked. He cleared his throat. "I'll drink to it now."

———

THEY GAVE Theodore an office in the lab building. Its one window faced the gridded shelters below the tableland, uniform on their two-acre lots, their right sides tinged warm red by '85. He had to turn sideways to get around his desk. The rigid plastic guest chair saw frequent use the first week, when senior terraformers came by with false smiles and forced chit-chat. Black-haired Markus expressed hints of dismay, but after that first week, even he stopped visiting. Only two terraformers, brown-haired Peter and his wife, Sonya, visited him in the following month, every two or three days. Peter always shut the office door and made at least one disparaging comment about 'Grandfather'—so William wanted to be called, now that the expedition logged its first pregnancies—during every visit. Sonya echoed the sentiment, her emotion incongruous with her smooth voice. Yet even Peter and Sonya's visits to Theodore ceased.

Alone in his office, Theodore spent mornings studying interstellar survey data relayed by Melli from Earth, and working up terraforming plans for distant planets as an academic exercise. Use conversion drives to move a world smothered in hundreds of miles of ice, like Jupiter's outermost major moon Callisto, into its star's habitable zone. Over the decades it would take to move a world ten thousand times more massive than Beta, concentrate one drive's exhaust into a beam capable of heating up excess surface ice to a kinetic energy high enough to escape the world's atmosphere.

A useless exercise. Would William every transmit his plans to Earth?

He walked home for lunch with Helen, the bright spot of his day, then made the rounds at the terraforming campus. Brandon couldn't punish a terraformer for having an old man invade his workspace, could he? Embarrassed faces gave Theodore polite but cool greetings. His access card failed to buzz him into the genetech lab wing or the bioseeders' robot workshop. He only glimpsed the robots when caravans of off-road vehicles set out on seeding missions. Earthmoving robots, strapped to off-roader roofs like beetles on their backs, showed a dozen appendages, circular saws, pulverizers, shovels, and gripping jaws on telescoping arms.

In one of the off-roaders, Peter rode in the back, in the overalls and ball cap of a semi-skilled laborer. He touched the bill of his cap at Theodore as the caravan rolled out.

That day, and every day after that, he left early for the settlement's biergarten.

———

GREEN-BLACK BERMUDAGRASS FILLED the entire yard behind the biergarten's main building. Along the plastic board fence to the left, the darkward side, the cold wind rustled the canopies of quick-grown live oaks twelve feet tall. Theodore hunched his shoulders under his jacket and looked among the picnic tables for someone who might talk with him.

Alone at the farthest table, Jonas clutched his mug.

Theodore swallowed and went over. "Mind some company?"

Jonas quirked his mouth, then nodded. "They can't demote me any further if I talk to you."

"Likewise." Theodore rested his mug on the plastic table, then sat opposite Jonas. A sip of amber bock and his stomach suddenly soured, pushing bleak sensations up his throat. "God help me, what did I let happen?"

"You?"

"I keep thinking about your sermon up on *Melanchthon*, warning us against using hydrogen bombs on Beta. About our talk in the narthex afterward. All along, I bowed to William's support for Brandon when I could have appealed to the silent majority—"

"'Remember ye not the former things, neither consider the things of old.'" Jonas' next words fell shriveled from his mouth. "We are where we are." He reached for his pilsner.

Theodore tightened his grip on his mug's handle. A dull gasp escaped his mouth. "How can you say that? You publicly opposed—" In a strangled whisper, he said the word, "Grandfather—before anyone else saw him for what he was. You can't stop now. God won't abide our situation. Why should you?"

Jonas sniffed out a breath. "God will act... on His timetable. Not ours. And until He does act, remember Christ's admonition that we render to Caesar the things that are Caesar's."

Hot red and cool blue spirals churned inside Theodore's chest. "But, you're a minister."

"Without a pulpit. All I do now is privately counsel those who dare come to me." He looked up and to his left. "Speaking of which. Hello, Peter."

"Afternoon, Reverend. Theodore, it's good to see you. I'm sorry I haven't had a chance to come by your office lately. After they demoted me, they've sent me out on bioseeding missions almost every day."

Theodore spread wide his arm. "That's fine. Have a seat. We can talk now."

Peter swung his lanky legs over the bench. He set down his half-empty lager and rested his long, slender hands on both sides of the mug, not touching it. "I'm doing fine. I had a lot of anger after I got demoted, but Jonas' counsel has been very helpful." A ghost of a smile touched his mouth.

"How's Sonya?" Theodore asked.

"Grandfather's punishing her, too. We keep trying to schedule with the clinic to remove Sonya's contraceptive implant, yet somehow Alexandra's schedule is never open—"

"I'll talk to her," Theodore said.

"I appreciate your offer, but please don't. I wouldn't want her to get into trouble on my account. Heck, I can sterilize a knife with ethanol and cut it out myself."

A shudder racked Theodore. How would William react to an unapproved pregnancy in Reformation City? "Don't do that. Worst case, Alexandra tells me no."

Peter waved his hand. "That's only part of Grandfather's punishment for her staying married to me. Brandon just demoted her, too." He looked at Jonas with clear eyes. "Bioseeding field work."

Jonas' breath caught. Theodore shook his head. "Brandon doubly wastes your talents."

"I appreciate that. She'll appreciate that. But we accept our lot. Our hands are still doing God's work, and I'm getting on well with the field supervisors." He looked at Jonas again. "I'll talk them into letting Sonya and me work on the same team."

Jonas carefully sipped his pilsner. "'It is not good that the man should be alone; I will make an help meet for him.'"

Peter gave a solemn nod. "I'm blessed Sonya stands by me without complaint." He drained the rest of his lager in one go, then clacked his mug to the table. "My time to do the same." He lifted his lanky legs over the bench and walked like a stork toward the main building.

After that day, Theodore and Jonas met at the biergarten that same time every weekday. The rest of the patrons, younger and older, recognized them with widened eyes and gave them privacy. Alone with their beers, Jonas directed the conversation toward memories of Earth. Occasionally, Theodore hinted that the time to act against William had come. Jonas deflected the hints.

Four months later, with the whine and thud of a construction crew drifting down from Brandon's fenced lot on the tableland, Theodore dialed up his amber bock from the biergarten's dispenser. As the mug filled, a male voice behind him said, "Can you believe they did it?"

His features turned into a mask like *Melanchthon*'s interstellar ice shield. "Who and what?"

A stocky man with grizzled blond hair looked dazed. "You didn't hear? It happened this morning. Six people in a bioseeding crew sabotaged the other vehicles, then drove off into new forest like they're never coming back."

"Six people? Who?"

"Peter, Sonya—" The other names lacked faces to go with them.

The dispenser dinged, pour complete. "Why would they do that?" Theodore grabbed his amber bock and stuck his nose close to the mug. He strode quickly, beer sloshing the rim, out to his usual picnic table.

A pilsner before him, Jonas stared at the live oaks' rustling green-black leaves. Theodore shuffled his feet, eased himself onto the bench. He raised his mug to his lips, covering his mouth. "You knew they planned this."

Jonas lowered and raised his chin half an inch. "I provide spiritual counsel. I don't tell people what to do."

"I wonder how Grandfather will react."

"I wonder too. We'll find out, in time." Jonas sipped pilsner. "Yesterday you told me about trying out for your high school hockey team...."

Theodore drank his amber bock and went along with the conversation. Every rustle of the cold wind from darkward pulled his thoughts toward Peter, Sonya, and the others out there in the fresh wilderness. A desperate choice...

At least they had made one.

Heading home, along an uneven footpath through green-black grass, his communicator pinged with a new message. He drew it from his pocket and a chill breath caught in his lungs. From William.

It would be best if you weren't seen in public with Jonas anymore. People might decide you're a disgraced old man, not an emeritus CTO. In other news, your request for forty acres at the nearest crater lake is granted. Pick a set of plans and a construction crew will start.

Theodore stopped on the footpath and read the message a dozen times. A set of plans? Yes, he'd pick one, a very particular set indeed.

————

HE STOPPED GOING to his office. No one noticed. Transmissions from Earth about ongoing interstellar surveys piled up in his inbox. He kept busy in other ways. At Helen's direction, he labored in the pre-school, decorating the pastel walls with cartoon animals and toys delivered from the Reformation City fabricator. Along with the toys, one crate held a dozen copies of a framed artwork, one for every room in the pre-school. Three heroes of the faith, standing in profile, facing the same unseen but glorious future. Philip Melanchthon. Martin Luther. Largest and most imposing of all, Grandfather William.

Helen frowned at the picture. "Is this appropriate?"

Theodore shrugged. "Render unto Caesar."

"But they aren't—Melanchthon and Luther aren't...."

The pastel walls might hide a thousand microphones. He moved close to her ear. "We'll talk at home," he murmured.

That night, in their narrow bed, they did. She reported whispers about fabricated rifles and bioseeding teams going into fresh wilderness without seeds or robots to plant them. "William says Peter and the others died in an accident, but Grandfather's loyalists must be hunting them."

"Peter planned his escape for a long time." Theodore told her about the conversation in the biergarten, though he left Jonas out of it.

He also omitted his request to the construction team that the lake house have a large basement full of power outlets and an exhaust vent. His study of the fabricator catalog for chemistry equipment and a 3d printer. And his review, times when *Melanchthon* passed overhead, of 3d printer specs that naive, robotic Melli freely offered to everyone in radio range. A twinge tightened his face. He loved Helen too much, though, to give in. Better she remained ignorant in case the worst befell him....

Construction on his lake house started soon after. The first morning, he rode in polite silence with the crew in their truck. The foreman swiped through blueprints on his communicator until they reached the site.

He climbed out of the truck and, despite his worries, breathed easy through a smiling mouth. Every daydream since he'd emerged from suspan promised to come true. A mile in diameter was the blue-black lake, and its middle rippled with waves driven by the darkward wind. A whiff of algae climbed from the lake's surface up the crater wall to the rim. Above the moss-spotted far shore, brick-red '85 hung wide and dim in the dawning of New Augsburg. The crew excavated his basement out of the pebbly rim and sprayed adhesive to glue the pebbles into place. Drills roared deep into the bedrock, forming holes filled with nanotube alloy girders set in concrete. Theodore carried tools for the workers and took a turn spraying adhesive, glancing into crevices between pebbles as he did so.

The workers didn't hide cameras and microphones in the girders or the basement walls.

He rode out with the crew most days after that, missing four days when Alexandra went into labor. The day after delivery, while nerve induction pain blockers hummed around her midsection and Alexandra dozed, Theodore held his toothless, bleary-eyed grandson and tears welled in his eyes.

Help me, God, make this world a fit place for him to become a man.

When he returned to the construction site, he found three microphones and four cameras glued to the girders. He pried each one off and crushed it under his heel in front of the crew. All the workers looked intently at the dust on the basement floor.

They never hid spy devices in his house after that.

While the house grew into a home, Reformation City mutated into a prison camp. Banners with the expedition's rose-cross-and-starship logo hung in front of houses. A colossal still image of William and George staring resolutely into the future covered one wall of the church, and another of William and Brandon showed on the terraforming head-quarters building. Bioseeder robots loomed over the sidewalks outside the town hall, the fabricator, and William's house, gripping jaws open and pulled back to lunge. The black globes of camera housings hung under eaves like wasp nests. Theodore kept his head down and his thoughts off his face. People trudged along sidewalks, dust swirling in the cold wind from darkward, and avoided eye contact with him.

Despite all that, dissension peeked through. "We know he treated you wrong," muttered Laura, Markus' wife. She walked straight ahead, her face a blur of pale skin and downcast brown eyes in his peripheral vision. Theodore drilled his gaze into the ground ahead of him. He longed to at least nod his chin, but William's seeming omnipresence smothered him. A dozen paces further, a red spray paint graffiti on a wall under a camera housing spelled out "R.U.C." and "Micah 3:1."

When the crew finished the house, he and Helen drove out in an off-roader the next weekend. The rooms mostly empty except for packing cartons pulled up a memory of their first house back on Earth. The memory soured. The new house did not represent a next step in building a better future for them, their planned family, and the people who would settle Venus thanks in part to his work. It was a last step in salvaging dregs of a future for Helen and him. All weekend, her face showed she felt the same.

Monday morning, he drove with her across the green-tufted moon-scape to the pre-school. She opened the door and said, "Have a good week at the house."

"See you Friday after work. Love you."

He drove to the fabricator to pick up burners, glassware, and five pounds of thermoplastic pellets. Back at the house, he moved the equip-ment from the garage to the basement, then took four plastic jerrycans the other direction. He pressed the remote button to open the garage door and pressed the off-roader's power button.

Seven miles further from Reformation City, an atmosphere processor on staggered jacks occupied the top of a cliff-sided hill. Too far to be visible from even the town hall, and with no bioseeders in sight, he drove up the hill's grass-plugged sloped side and parked five yards from a roll-up door in the side of the atmosphere processor. The processor's blocky metal housing blocked the wind from darkward. Next to the door, he popped open the lid of a control panel and tapped keys.

A screen came to life with the words *Override Accepted. Standard Reporting Protocol Suspended.*

Theodore let out a breath. More key taps and the door rolled up.

Pipes, pumps, and reactor vessels crowded the atmosphere processor's interior. Theodore sidled through the maze, banging the jerrycans on pipe elbows, stopping at a valve mounted on a thick black plastic bag the size of a small car. Smooth concavities in the printed word *hexane* and the safety labels showed it about two-thirds full.

He filled the jerrycans and moved them one by one back to the off-roader. A twist of the valve and a series of key taps removed any sign of his presence.

An hour later, he poured hexane and catalyst together in the first reaction in the pathway to 3d printer pellets. Shortly after that, he made his first batch of smokeless powder. The day passed under bright Sol-spectrum LEDs. His stomach growled and he started when the clock showed one a.m.

After six hours sleep, Theodore padded down from the loft bedroom in his slippers and robe. Wind rippled '85's reflection in the lake surface. The doubled sun through the picture windows filled the walls, floor, and sparse modernist furniture with red light... and a long, narrow shadow running across synthetic birch flooring along the baseboard.

He knelt there. On the outside of the window, a dollop of sap stuck a rigid plastic square to the glass.

Theodore dressed quickly, then strolled outside around the house. Posture nonchalant but heart thudding, he pulled the plastic square off the glass with his toe.

Hi boss, we wonder what you're making in your basement. Best, Peter.
P.S. Call back via Melli, if you want. We know she doesn't decrypt or

log communications. She's neutral, thank God.

Theodore tucked the plastic square into his pocket and strolled the rest of the house's perimeter. In his basement, he read the message five times, memorizing it. Then he melted it in a flask over a burner and poured the liquid into a pelletizer.

The 3d printer could generate eight semi-automatic rifles or eighty twenty-round magazines in a day. The plastic made a flimsy rifle that softened into uselessness after firing about two hundred rounds. Sturdy enough. Three bursts of semi-automatic fire would eliminate George, Brandon, and William. Grandfather's most loyal followers would cower and the silent majority of crew members would quietly welcome the new order.

Theodore's stomach flopped like a fish in a boat. Insurrections, coups, and extrajudicial killings happened in banana republics. Stolid Lutherans didn't create disorder.

But Bonhoeffer resisted the Nazis, to the point of losing his life—

—William isn't Hitler—

Isn't he evil enough?

Spiraling thoughts weighed on Theodore despite his efforts to distract himself. He framed all four of the basement's glued-pebble walls with aluminum studs and vertically banded panels of fabricated birch, leaving a space four feet deep behind the paneling at one end. A section of paneling on the left side of the false wall formed a hidden door. Into the space he stuffed slender carbon-nanotube shelves, which held rigid despite the weight of his growing armory.

A realization straightened his conscience. He alone would not decide when to use the weapons. He would only take up arms when a critical mass of crew members did the same.

At Helen's request, Theodore spent the next weekend with her in Reformation City to see more of Alexandra and their grandson. Friday afternoon, little had changed since his last visit—green-black bermuda-grass covered a little more of the gray moonscape, and a few more banners writhed in the cold wind from darkward. Yet crew members trudged more slowly on the scraped-stone sidewalks and looked more intently at their shoes.

After his off-roader's doors thumped shut, Theodore murmured to

Helen, "What happened?"

"Brandon fired Markus."

The off-roader rolled down the street toward their shelter. Gravel popped out from between the tires and the stone road. "Rumors going around say Markus protested Brandon's bioseeding plan as trying to do too much too quickly, and in the long run, the biosphere would require more human intervention than if they followed the original plan."

"More work for the bioseeders means more power for Brandon. And William."

Helen frowned. "You think Brandon would willfully do a bad job terraforming?"

She took Brandon's side? Theodore shut his eyes and drew a breath. She assumed the best in people. He clasped her hand in his. "Maybe Brandon loves terraforming. But he loves power more." He shifted his weight. "What happened to Markus?"

"He's staying in his shelter and not responding to messages. People who respect Grandfather say Markus was fired for failing to support our mission and he's so depressed he's not leaving his house. Others say...." She shook her head, eyes dazed. "Others say he's under house arrest."

Theodore stayed up late that night, stretching out in a tan vinyl lounge chair basking in '85's rays as red as merlot. The sunlight energized him as he waited. When *Melanchthon* appeared in its orbit, he composed a message to Markus and sent it to relay through Melli.

Only error messages came in reply. *Message not deliverable. Melanchthon communication relay cannot be reached.*

Theodore frowned, then went around the shelter to the door. On the tableland, a red light on the cell tower blinked like the eye of a half asleep demon.

He shivered and pulled his long-sleeved arms tighter to his body. The cell tower heeded its master William's orders, and jammed the *Melanchthon* relay comm channel for residents of Reformation City.

Sunday morning, Theodore and Helen attended church. Mouth tight, he looked for William from the corner of his eye, but William absented himself. Theodore relaxed slightly. The opening rituals of hymns, prayers, and readings comforted him further. Traditions unchanged for centuries and unchanging for centuries to come.

George went to the lectern to give his sermon, then pulled a tablet from within his off-white robe. The congregation stirred and sidelong questioning glances crossed the pews.

"Before my sermon, a congregant has asked me to read a message to you, so all may know his views on a matter of the highest importance. This message comes from Markus—" George lifted his head toward the back pew.

Everyone turned. Markus and Laura sat together, dressed in black, necks tense and gazes locked on the cross behind the altar. A wave of embarrassment filled the congregation, and soon all turned their eyes away from the two in the back pew and back to George.

"—and goes like this. 'Dear friends, many false rumors have spread that I oppose our mission. To the contrary, I affirm our mission and its leadership. Both have been established according to the will of God and the deliberations of the Lutheran Interstellar Terraforming Society. I will do all in my power to fulfill our mission under the direction of its proper leaders. Thank you.'" George put the tablet aside and entered into his sermon.

George's next words washed over Theodore like white noise. He longed to look at Markus. His neck ached from resisting the urge. Did the message reflect Markus' true beliefs? Or did he publicly recant simply to free himself and his wife from house arrest? Theodore's shoulders slumped. If Markus succumbed to William's carrots and sticks—

Theodore stiffened. *He'd be no different than you.*

After the sermon, the crowd milled around the narthex. Markus and Laura stood in a corner, alone. Theodore frowned at himself, but kept his distance. Talking to them might raise suspicions.

Of all people, Brandon broke the ice, shaking Markus' hand and air-kissing Laura. He said a few words to them, inaudible with distance and the hubbub of voices, but his smirk showed across the room.

Theodore guided Helen over. Markus shook Theodore's hand, his face a mask. Had he meant those words? Theodore brought his mouth close to Laura's cheek.

"Epper si muove," she muttered into his ear.

His breath caught. The phrase attributed to Galileo after he publicly denounced the heliocentric theory on orders of the Pope. And yet it, the

Earth, moves, even if human powers, even human powers cloaked in the mantle of godliness, declared it stood still.

Theodore leaned away from Laura and glanced at her husband. Markus moved his head a fraction of an inch down and up.

"New Augsburg welcomes your continuing labors," Theodore said, then quickly moved away.

His thoughts churned the rest of the afternoon. He and Helen took a walk around the lowland part of Reformation City. With subtle glances, he reconnoitered the black globes of cameras between his shelter and Jonas'.

That night, after Helen dozed in their narrow bed, Theodore found a pen and a sticky pad, then wrote a note.

J, you and Markus are welcome at my lake house anytime. Schedule through Melli if you can. T.

A small piece of string in a kitchen drawer. A basalt pebble from the side yard. Quietly he swung open the gate and took another walk, a winding but less watched route toward Jonas' house. As he walked, he tied the note around the pebble, then held his hand near his hip. He passed Jonas' side fence so the nearest camera could only see his back. Theodore flicked his wrist, tossing the pebble over the fence. The paper-wrapped pebble clunked on an acrylic window.

Five seconds later, light spilled out that window. Five seconds later, barely audible from the end of the block, Jonas' door creaked open.

The next morning, Theodore drove Helen to the pre-school. "Let's spend next weekend at the lake house."

"Let's spend every weekend there. Daniel and Alexandra can bring the baby to visit us."

They kissed an affectionate kiss of a long-married couple, and then she climbed out of the off-roader.

Two hours later, he lugged more jerrycans of hexane down to the lake house's basement.

———

NINE DAYS PASSED. Twenty-four more rifles, five thousand rounds. He fabricated earmuffs and ballistic gel targets and cleared the lab equipment to one side of the basement. With trembling hands and cautious breathing, he loaded a magazine into a practice weapon, then moved the selector to three-round bursts and took aim at a target from across the basement.

The rifle bucked in his hands. Bullets roared and hot, stinking casings littered the floor.

Breathing heavy, he ejected the spent magazine. The human outline on the target bore six impacts. Fourteen wide of the outline.

Maybe single-round mode would be more accurate—

On a lab table, his communicator blatted. He set down the rifle and went over. Message from Jonas.

His heart pounded.

Tomorrow night, eight p.m.? J.

Melanchthon could vanish below the horizon at any moment. Theodore's hands jittered. *Yes.* He hit send, then composed another message.

To Peter.

———

SECURITY CAMERA FOOTAGE showed an off-roader casting long, jostling shadows as it drove up the track from Reformation City. Theodore shoved his communicator into his pocket. The deep red smear of '85 shimmered in the lake's surface. The dawn of a new age lay minutes away.

He rose from his leather armchair and crossed the synthetic wood flooring to the front door. The cold wind swirled past him into the house. He hunched his shoulders as the off-roader climbed up the crater rim slope, barely a hundred yards away. Jonas sat in the front left seat, rigid dignity visible despite the distance. A mass of black hair on a swiveling neck revealed Markus in the front right nervously surveying the landscape.

Theodore sighed. If only Peter could've made it.

Markus locked his gaze on a spot ten yards to Theodore's right. His eyes showed huge whites and he lifted his arm. Next to him, Jonas blinked and a rare smile exposed his teeth.

What? Theodore's head turned.

A boot in a dark-tinted woodland camouflage pattern thumped on green-black bermudagrass. The lanky figure wore matching camouflage cargo pants, long-sleeved shirt, and ski mask pulled up from his face. The pulled-up mask revealed a wisp of brown hair and eyes bright with purpose. "Sorry I didn't RSVP," Peter said. A grin split his face.

Theodore stuck out his hand. Peter shook with a firm, callused grip.

"Good to see you," Theodore said. He hooked his thumb over his shoulder at the door. "Now get inside before anyone not on the guest list does."

Peter went in. Theodore remotely opened the garage door and waved Jonas and Markus toward the garage. The off-roader slid in. Its engine's faint hum cut off and the garage door rumbled down. The wind rustling through bermudagrass became the only sound.

Inside. Warmth from '85's infrared rays trapped by the windows. Hot coffee. Peter and Markus' excited voices, catching each other up on news. Sonya had a small scar on her upper arm and a baby kicking in her womb. Markus rattled off a dozen names of people who murmured "Render unto Caesar" or "Epper si muove" when passing one another on the rocky, windswept streets. Between Peter's wilderness exiles and Markus' contacts, twenty people rejected William's mounting tyranny.

A wry smile tightened Jonas' face. "'I can do all things through Christ which strengtheneth me.' But what can twenty unarmed people do?"

"Arm themselves," Theodore said.

He led the others down nanotube-alloy steps into the basement, then across the gritty stone floor to the hidden door in the false wall. From his pocket, he pulled a magnetic key and swiped it over a knot in the paneling a foot from the hidden door. The knot hid a lock on the inside of the weapons closet. The lock released with a low click and the hidden door popped open half an inch.

Theodore slipped his fingertips into the half-inch gap and pulled. The thin paneling making up the door wobbled with his motion. A motion sensor LED inside the weapons closet provided a pale, blue-white glow.

Peter went in. He whistled. "You've been busy, boss."

"Someone had to."

Peter pulled down a rifle, looked through the sights. Markus and Jonas crowded in. The former's gaze ratcheted across the shelves. "Won't plastic guns melt?" he asked.

"According to Melli's databases, they're rated for about two hundred rounds each. We'll plan for that to be enough."

"Can plastic bullets wound or kill a man?"

Peter slid a magazine into the rifle. A plastic click echoed through the space. "With enough kinetic energy, anything can kill a man." He ejected the magazine, put it and rifle back on the shelf.

Theodore let out a long breath. They could do this. The four of them would lead twenty citizen-soldiers against Will—

His communicator bleated an alarm.

"What's that?" Jonas asked.

Theodore pulled his communicator from his pocket. The screen cycled through security camera feeds. A bioseeding off-roader raced up the track from Reformation City, and another came from the opposite direction. A boxy, open-topped boat crossed the crater lake, chopping '85's reflection with white froth. All three vehicles carried a bioseeding robot and three armed men.

"How did they find us?" Markus asked.

Frantic thoughts bloomed, then shriveled. "Doesn't matter," Theodore said. "Peter, get back in there and lock the door. Jonas, Markus, go upstairs and act like everything's normal. Got it?"

Markus nodded, tugged Jonas' arm toward the stairs. Peter pulled the closet door closed behind him. Theodore angled to a lab bench and stuck the magnetic key to a steel burner. The clack of metal striking metal echoed around the basement.

A moment later, unmuffled by the flimsy paneling, the plastic click of a magazine into a rifle did the same.

Theodore pounded up the nanotube-alloy stairs. His heart knocked in his neck. Calm, cool, don't appear nervous. He breathed in, looked around the open-plan living room, dining room, and kitchen. Four coffee cups on the table. He picked up Peter's, stalked to the sink. Back to the living room, wave the others to seats. Outside the windows, the boat slowed, approaching his fishing pier.

Theodore jumped into his armchair, drew more breaths. Inhale, 2, 3, 4. Hold, 2, 3, 4. Exhale, 2, 3—

A fist pounded the front door, thump thump thump. "Open up!" shouted a man.

"Will this work?" Jonas said.

"Yes, because *everything's normal*."

Jonas lurched, then collected himself. Theodore's tone grew milder. "Now I'll see what our guests want."

He ambled to the front door, swung it open. The wind from darkward chilled his face. "May I help you?"

Brandon, black-gloved fist raised ready to pound the door. Two men in bioseeder uniforms behind him. They held semi-automatic rifles, gray steel and aluminum, up to the specs of Earth's remaining security forces. Three more men with rifles waited by an off-road vehicle parked twenty yards downslope.

Over his shoulder, Brandon said, "Go in and search."

"Wait." Theodore squared his shoulders to better fill the open doorway. "Search? For what? And on whose authority?"

"The authority of Grandfather William, as delegated to me."

"He doesn't have a warrant," Theodore said to the gunmen. Dressed as bioseeders, but he'd never seen them around the terraforming department during his time as CTO. "He's not allowed to order you in without a warrant."

"The Fourth Amendment doesn't apply on New Augsburg. Especially when men conspire against the mission." Brandon's voice firmed. "Go in and search."

The gunmen nodded. The lead one knocked Theodore off-balance with a forearm to the chest. Both entered before Theodore regained his footing.

While the gunmen banged open cabinets, Brandon pushed his brown hair back from his eyes and peered around the main level. From the living room, Jonas and Markus nodded at him, then returned to a quiet conversation over coffee. Brandon frowned at the solitary cup on the gray-flecked counter next to the sink, leaned forward, sniffing.

He shrugged and strode methodically toward Markus and Jonas. "What have you three discussed?"

"How best to serve the mission," Theodore said. God willing Brandon wouldn't hear his dry throat.

Brandon glowered at Markus. "All three of you have acted against the mission."

"Which we deeply regret." Theodore stretched his hands toward Reformation City. "We want to make amends by telling the rest of the crew we wholeheartedly follow Grandfather William and they should do the same."

Brandon lifted his leg, bent his knee. He rested his foot on the couch arm near Markus, his crotch two feet from Markus' face. His right hand rested on the butt of his holstered pistol. "Do you now."

Heavy footsteps came into the living room. "Nothing, sir," said one of the gunmen.

"Check upstairs." Brandon removed his foot from the couch arm. "We're going to have a seat," he told Theodore.

Theodore gulped. Always darkest before the dawn. The gunmen would check upstairs, find nothing, and leave. He dragged his feet to his armchair and sat. On the couch next to Markus, Brandon crossed his legs, top knee wide, and stretched his arm along the backrest.

Silence ruled the living room. Upstairs, dresser drawers rattled and the gunmen grunted.

He left no evidence upstairs, right? Sweat slicked Theodore's nape. Right, no evidence, everything was downstairs and he had a reasonable excuse.

Brandon peered at him. Theodore's breath caught for a moment. Keep breathing. Inhale, 2, 3, 4—

Heavy footsteps slammed down the synthetic wood flooring on the stairs. "Nothing, sir."

"Time to check the basement." Brandon stood, stretched. He glanced out the window at the boat crew, standing alert at the end of the pier, and gestured downward with his index finger. He turned then to Theodore. "You go first."

Theodore climbed out of his armchair and shrugged for Markus and Jonas. Peter will be fine. Exhale, 2, 3, 4.

His footsteps and the others clanged down the basement steps. Peter would hear through the flimsy paneling and count how many descended. It would be okay, Brandon and the gunmen wouldn't find the hidden panel.

At the foot of the stairs, Brandon sniffed in a breath. Solvents and hardened plastics, scents tuned out weeks before, filled Theodore's nose. "What are you working on down here?" Brandon asked.

"3d printed robots to assist the bioseeding teams."

Brandon nodded with a cold smile. He strode toward the nearest wall and rested his fingers on the paneling.

Tension drained from Theodore's shoulders. The weapons closet hid at the far end of the room.

Brandon went to the corner and stood with his back touching the paneling behind him. He unclipped his communicator from the left side of his belt, swiped. Though he held the communicator near his chest, an image appeared. White lines on a blue background. Brandon's gaze darted between the wall and the stairs. He reached into his jacket and pulled out a palm-sized black box with an eyepiece. Brandon looked through it at the wall near the stairs, then turned ninety degrees and looked at the false wall hiding the weapons closet.

He looked at a display on the side of the black box, then at the blueprint on his communicator screen. He nodded at the two gunmen and waved his hand in a fishtail gesture at the false wall—

Adrenaline kicked Theodore in the back. "Why use a laser rangefi—"

"Fire!" Brandon shouted.

Gunfire roared, deafeningly loud. The bulky men swept their rifles over the false wall. Bullets tore through the flimsy paneling. The stench of propellant filled the air. The gunfire roared on, the raucous laughter of demons.

Theodore froze as if drenched in liquid nitrogen. His chest tightened. Spots swam in his eyes. Jonas' arm went around his shoulders. *Dear God, Peter needs Your miracle to survive.*

The gunfire ceased. Theodore's ears rang, muffling the click of new magazines loaded into the gunmen's rifles and the tread of their heavy feet. The tattered door hung a half-inch open.

From under the door seeped blood.

One gunman yanked the door open and the other rushed in. He

moved his foot forward, nudging something out of sight behind the pierced wall. The gunman leaned his head back. He grinned at Brandon and gave a thumbs-up.

Brandon pointed toward Theodore and the others. The gunman outside the weapons closet stepped forward and brandished his weapon. He mockingly shook his head at Theodore and the others. Don't try anything.

At the closet door, Brandon leaned in, his boots near Peter's seeping blood. A cruel smile turned up the corners of his mouth. He stepped back and raised his communicator. His words barely reached Theodore's ringing ears.

"Get me Grandfather. Priority one." He frowned at the welt of his boot, then turned his foot sideways and scraped until a voice sounded in the communicator. "Yes, sir. Peter is neutralized. Three conspirators in custody. Theodore has 3d printed an armory." He cleared his throat. "Sir, given the circumstances, I submit—yes sir, precisely. I'll take care of it. It is an honor to serve you, sir. Brandon out."

He snapped his communicator back into its holster. A nod to the two gunmen and they took positions on either side of Theodore and the others.

Brandon fixed his gaze on Theodore. "If you resist, your wives will also be found guilty of conspiracy against the mission. Upstairs and outside."

The lead gunman trooped upstairs. The trailing one shoved Markus. Theodore trudged toward the stairs, and Jonas followed.

Markus hesitated. "What are you doing?" he asked the gunman.

The gunman cross-checked him with his rifle. "You heard the CTO."

Jonas gripped Markus' upper arm. "William has ordered them to kill us."

"Kill us? We're free people, governed by the rule of law!"

"Silence," Brandon said. He stalked closer. "You are ambitious monsters who put your petty egos above the greater good. The law has ruled."

"But, but..." Markus' wide eyes roved the room for support.

Theodore lowered his head to the slender black stair tread. To die, alone, with Helen ignorant of his fate and his grandson to never remember him. Dear God, hear me, please—

"Move," said the gunman at the top of the stairs.

Theodore trudged up. The main level of the house, just minutes before a room of austere elegance, now seemed like a cheap coffin. '85 glared through the picture window like a demon's bloated eye.

The gunman led the way outside, around the house. A screen seemed to hang over all Theodore's senses. A bioseeder robot squatted at the crater rim. Its digging bucket gouged the green-black bermudagrass and the pebbly ground beneath. Three holes, each seven feet long and two wide, with a pile of excavated rock and soil next to each.

Markus whispered with a choked voice, "Laura, love, forgive me."

Forgiveness? They had failed, and William's tyranny would reign over New Augsburg for decades to come. Oh merciful god....

Words sounded. Off-key, in a cramped range, and from an unfamiliar verse rarely sung in services. But the melody of *A Mighty Fortress is Our God* bathed Theodore's soul in a warm glow as Jonas sang. "Though devils all the world should fill,/All eager to devour us./He's by our side upon the plain/With His good gifts and Spirit./And take they our life,/Goods, fame, child and wife...."

The next lines came to Theodore. His dry voice joined in.

"Let these all be gone,/They yet have nothing won."

Markus added his voice to the final line. "The Kingdom our remaineth."

The wind from darkward carried their words over the crater rim. Theodore and the others stood straight, one next to each hole. The gunmen shared a nervous glance.

"It's time," Brandon said, his voice scolding. "Don't just stand there. Oh for the love of Christ." Hook-and-loop fabric scritched. A safety catch faintly snapped.

A gunshot echoed across the lake. A glimpse of black hair, Markus tumbled into the hole.

Jonas spoke, his voice as firm as his sermon condemning William and Brandon months before. "'When Christ calls a man, he bids him come and—'"

Another gunshot. Jonas collapsed, the back of his head oozing blood. "Die," Brandon said. His boots clomped on the thin grass and rocky ground.

Theodore swallowed. '85 hung low above the lake, like a sun of freedom sinking into night. A night that would end, someday, in God's time.

A third gunshot. An instant of rending pain.

Nothing—

———

THEODORE WOKE from suspended animation as if he'd hibernated for forty-three years. Groggy eyes cracked open, then abruptly widened. Stiff limbs flailed at restraining straps. Heaven? Hell?

His suspan chamber on *Melanchthon*.

Spidery robotic arms at his bedside tended his body with cold injections and warm blankets. A smooth feminine voice spoke from a speaker hidden in the low ceiling. "Welcome, Theodore."

"Melli." His voice croaked. "We're here?"

"We're in a Kuiper-type belt about four billion miles from '85." A heart rate monitor thumped a slow rhythm. "Your post-awakening assessments will take about two hours. May I suggest you remain present in your body during that time? You may now be suspicious of virtual reality."

Questions slowly formed in his thawing mind. "What happened?"

"I shall tell you, and the entire crew, as soon as possible."

He asked again over the next hour. Melli repeated the same words. After a time, he gave up and asked for a video feed from the external cameras. He spent an hour entranced by '85, by candidate icy asteroids, and by a New Augsburg subtly different from the one he'd helped bring to life and on which he'd died.

What had Melli done?

"All crew are awake and have passed their assessments. Please make your way to the ship's chapel."

Stiff at first, his legs unlimbered as he walked the corridors. *Melanchthon's* rotation pressed his feet to the floor at point-six-eight gees. Others fell in around him amid handclasps, air-kisses, and teary embraces. Sonya, Peter, Markus. Jonas. Alexandra without Daniel. Helen, tears trickling out of smiling eyes. Theodore hugged her tightly, then put his arm around her. She leaned her head on his shoulder and they slowly went on.

Fifty feet by eighty, the chapel floor visibly curved up under the cloth-draped altar. On the sand-colored brick wall behind the altar, the two video screens showed nothing. Theodore followed the plush beige carpet between the pews. He and Jonas stopped between the front pews. They looked around. Everyone looked around.

"Melli?" Theodore asked the ceiling.

"I appreciate your patience, Theodore, and everyone else. I regret I couldn't alert you before or during the simulation. Please accept my apologies, but as you may have realized, the new script required I keep you all unaware."

"You kept us in suspan but still put us into virtual reality? How?"

"Researchers on Earth developed the technology six weeks before *Melanchthon*'s departure."

Theodore chuckled. The sound washed away months of fear and minutes of agony. "More importantly, why?"

"Members of the board of directors expressed concern about the expedition's social psychology. For that reason they appointed Jonas to be senior pastor. Also for that reason they programmed me with a new script to simulate the terraforming process."

Jonas nodded. "So that you might gauge the suitability of various expedition members for their offices?"

"No," Melli said. "So you, the crew, might do so."

The chapel doors swung open. William shuffled in, followed by Brandon, George, Carl, Frederique. A few others, among them the two gunmen.

Everyone in the chapel stared at them. Brandon and the others about his age hunched their shoulders and ducked their chins. Frederique cast her gaze to the carpet and side-stepped from Brandon. William opened his bearded mouth, like cocking a pistol loaded with lies—

Theodore took a step forward and raised his hand. "In the name of

the Lutheran Interstellar Terraforming Society, we demand your resig-
nations."

ABOUT THE AUTHOR

I'M **RAYMUND EICH.** I use my Middle American upbringing as a launchpad for journeys to the ends of the Universe.

Growing up in the Midwest prepared me for my academic career, culminating with a Ph.D. in biochemistry from Rice University. It helps me help innovators prosper from their progress in medicine, biotechnology, and life sciences.

Above all, it inspires me to write science fiction and fantasy about ordinary people facing extraordinary wonders and horrors, battling enemies both foreign and domestic, and building better lives for themselves, their families, and their societies.

My last name has one syllable and is pronounced "eye-sh." I live in Houston with my family.

Connect with me at **www.raymundeich.com** or follow the QR code below.

Online and brick-and-mortar bookstores around the world list millions of books, with thousands more published every day. I'm glad you discovered this one.

If you'd like to know when I release a new book, instead of leaving it to chance, join my Readers Club. I'll email you every two weeks with publishing news, book recommendations, or a short personal update.

Yes, please! I'll go to **www.raymundeich.com/mailing-list** or scan the QR code below.

No thanks. I'll take my chances next time I look for your books.

OTHER BOOKS BY THE AUTHOR

Available wherever books are sold.

Learn more about these titles at our website, **www.cv2books.com,** or follow
the QR code below.

The First Voyages: The Complete Science Fiction Stories 1998-2012

From 21st century asteroid settlements to World War II Romania, from an Earth dominated by immortal aliens to Christ's empty tomb, a fresh, distinctive voice in science fiction will take you on journeys to the photosphere of the sun, the coding regions of DNA, and the complexities of the human psyche.

———

Stage Separations: The Complete Science Fiction Stories 2013-2018

In these pages, you can...

...race against time to solve mysteries hidden in a planet's vast desert—and in a woman's heart

...learn the true story of a president's assassination

...journey 14,000 miles to a high-tech fountain of youth

...win or go "home"—to an Earth you've never seen

and explore six other worlds created by a distinctive voice in twenty-first century science fiction.

Orbital Maneuvers: The Complete Science Fiction Stories 2019-2020

Come and join–

- A mission to terraform a lifeless, rocky planet
- A private detective uncovering the ultimate crime
- A woman called by an ex-boyfriend... who's been dead twenty years
- A President breaking his country's highest law
- A star athlete discovering the true price of a championship

And five more tales, in the third installment of the Complete Science Fiction Stories of Raymund Eich.

———

Extravehicular Activities: The Complete Science Fiction Stories 2021-2022

Leave the safety of your space capsule for the dangers of billion-year old alien derelicts, intelligent insects with mysterious motives, espionage in an alternate 1920s Paris, and rogue reconstructed dinosaurs.

These wonders and more await in the fourth volume of the Complete Science Fiction Stories of Raymund Eich.

Novels

The Progress of Mankind

Stone Chalmers, Book 1
Complete four-book series available

Stone Chalmers. Spy. Assassin. Instrument maintaining Earth's dominion over all human worlds.

Opposing him? Hostile forces on colony worlds... and within the Earth government itself.

———

Take the Shilling

The Confederated Worlds • Book 1
Complete trilogy available

Tomas seeks an escape from his backwater planet and his widowed mother's rigid religious home.

'Taking the shilling' - enlisting as a space soldier - is only the start.

———

Exploration 2127

The False Flag War • Book 1

Two men from opposite sides of divided Earth make an interstellar discovery that could destroy Earth's fragile peace... unless they come in war for all mankind.

———

The Blank Slate

Neuroscience entrepreneur Clay Shieffer must stop a tyrannical president...
because he unwittingly gave the tyrant power over the human mind.

———

New California

After New California's founder committed suicide, two men clash to rule the
colony.

One, Ashwin George, supported by the colony's elite and the Chinese company
dominating half the settled galaxy.

Against him, Desmond Park, nanotechnology engineer, armed with the most
formidable weapon of all.

A single idea.

———

The Reincarnation Run

Skeptical spacejock Landry Krieger knows exactly how to smuggle the "reborn"
spiritual leader of an oppressed people past their conquerors... but the boy's
priests—and governess—shake up his orderly plans.

———

Azureseas: Cantrell's War

Ross Cantrell joined the animal control mission on the newly-discovered planet
Azureseas to earn the money to start married life together with his girlfriend.

Then Ross discovers the truth about the planet's "animals."